contents

FOLLOW THE
SWALLOW

Illustrated by Martin Ursell

For Helen

J.D.

For Anne

M.U.

Chack the blackbird was learning to fly.

So was Apollo the swallow.

That was how they met.

'Who are you?' asked Chack.

'I'm Apollo. I'm a swallow.'

'And what do you swallow?'

'Flies, mostly,' said Apollo. 'And

who are you?'

I'm Apollo!

'I'm Chack. I'm a blackbird.'

'You look brown to me,' said Apollo.

'I may be brown now but one day I'll

be black,' said Chack.

'I don't believe you!' said Apollo.

Apollo showed Chack his nest. It was

on a cobwebby shelf in a shed.

'I won't always live here,' he said.

'One day I'll fly away to Africa.'

'I don't believe you!' said Chack.

Chack showed Apollo his nest.

It was in a tree covered in white blossom.

'One day the tree will be covered in tasty orange berries,' said Chack.

'I don't believe you!' said Apollo.

The days grew longer and warmer. Apollo started going around with a lot of other swallows. They kept gathering on the roof of the shed and then flying off all together.

'What are you doing?' asked Chack.

'Practising flying to Africa!' said Apollo.

'I don't believe you!' said Chack.

The white blossom fell off Chack's tree

and some little green berries appeared.

'They'll be orange one day,' he told Apollo.

'I don't believe you!'

said Apollo.

Slowly the berries on the tree grew bigger and changed colour, from green . . . to yellow . . . and at last to orange.

'Now Apollo will believe me!' said Chack. He flew to the shed to tell his friend about the orange berries.

'Come to the tree! Come to the tree!' he called.

I can't wait to show Apollo!

But Apollo had gone! He and the other swallows had just set off for Africa.

Chack flew after the swallows. He flew
and he flew till he reached the sea.
There he met a jumpy dolphin.

'Can you take a message to Apollo the swallow from Chack the blackbird?' asked Chack. 'He's on his way to Africa.'

'What is the message?' asked the dolphin.

'Come to the tree!' said Chack, and he

flew back to eat some of the tasty orange

berries.

The jumpy dolphin swam and leapt and
dived.

It took him a long time to reach Africa.

There he met a grumpy camel.

'Can you take a message to Apollo the swallow from Chack the blackbird?' asked the dolphin.

Hey, grumpy!

'What's the message?' asked the camel.

'Er . . . er . . . "Jump in the sea!"' said the dolphin.

The grumpy camel trudged slowly across the desert . . .

. . . till he reached a wide river. There he met a greedy crocodile.

'Can you take a message to Apollo the swallow from Chack the blackbird?' asked the camel.

'What's the message?' asked the crocodile.

'Er . . . er . . . "Grumpy like me!"' said the camel.

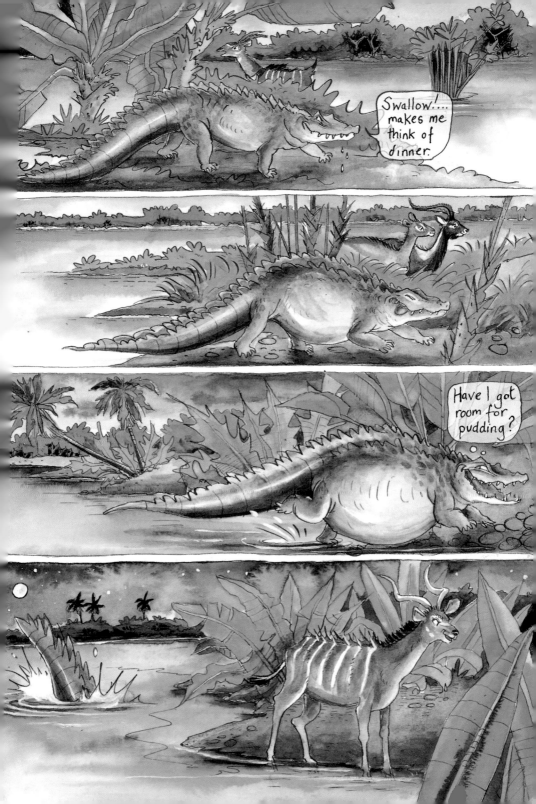

The greedy crocodile took his time

swimming and snapping his way down

the river . . .

. . . till he came to a forest. There he met

a playful monkey.

'Can you take a message to Apollo

the swallow from Chack the blackbird?'

asked the crocodile.

Monke
for te

'What is the message?' asked the monkey.

Er. . . er . . . "Monkey for tea!"' said the crocodile.

The playful monkey swung from branch

to branch till he came to a fig tree . . .

On the ground lay a lot of rotten figs.

Feeding on the rotten figs were a lot of

fruitflies, and snapping at the fruitflies

were a lot of swallows.

'I've got a message for Apollo the

swallow,' said the monkey.

'That's me!' said one of the swallows.

'What is the message and who is it from?'

'It's from Chack the blackbird and the message is . . . er, er, "One, two, three, whee!"' said the monkey.

'One, two, three, whee!' said Apollo.

'That's a funny message! Well, I've been in Africa for half a year now. It's time for me to fly back to the garden. I can find out what Chack means.'

Apollo and the other swallows flew back,

over the forest . . .

and the river . . .

and the desert . . .

Monkey for tea...

Grumpy like me!

and the sea . . .

. . . till they reached the garden. Apollo

flew to Chack's tree. It was covered in

white blossom.

A big blackbird flew down from the tree.

'I'm looking for my friend Chack,' said

Apollo.

'That's me!' said Chack.

'I don't believe you!'

said Apollo.

You're not Chack!

'You're black and Chack was brown.'

'I'm Chack as sure as eggs are eggs,'

said Chack. 'And talking of eggs, I've

got something to show you.'

He flew up to a nest in the tree. Apollo
flew after him. A brown bird was sitting
in the nest.

'Time for your worm-break, Rowena,'
said Chack.

The brown bird flew off, and there in the nest Apollo saw some pale, bluey-green eggs. He counted them . . . 'one, two, three. So the message wasn't "One, two, three, whee!" It was "One, two, three eggs!"' he said.

'No, it wasn't!' said Chack. 'It was

"Come to the tree!"'

'Well, I have come to the tree and I've

seen the eggs, and I think they're

beautiful,' said Apollo.

The message was. 'Come to the tree!'

'But the message wasn't about the eggs,
it was about the orange berries,' said Chack.
'Orange berries! Orange berries! You're
not still on about orange berries, are you?'
Apollo started to laugh.

'But there really were orange berries!'
said Chack. 'There were and there will
be again.'

Apollo thought hard.

'All right, then,' he said, ' I believe you.'

Do dh'Eleanor agus Mícheal
J.D.

To my spider-loving sisters,
Lyn and Angela
L.P.

Spinderella

Illustrated by Liz Pichon

46

The children of Scuttleton Primary School were eating their dinner – fish fingers, potatoes and peas. High up above them, on the ceiling of the dinner hall, the spiders of Scuttleton Primary School were eating their dinner – flies, flies and flies.

Delicious!

'How many flies have we got today, Mum?'
asked Spinderella, the smallest spider.

'Lots,' said Mum.

'Loads,' said her nine brothers and sisters,
with their mouths full.

'Loads isn't a number,' complained

Spinderella.

'Never mind about numbers. Eat up

your flies,' said her mum.

After dinner, the children went out
to play. Spinderella swung down
from the web like a yo-yo. She hung
there looking out of the window
into the playground.
'It's football!' she cried.

50

In a flash her mum and her nine
brothers and sisters were swinging
beside her. All the spiders' eyes were
fixed on the football game.

'What a tackle!' they cried, and,

'Go, go, go!'

Yippee!

Then, 'GOAL!' they all yelled. They clapped their spindly legs and nearly let go of their threads. The children scored goal after goal. 'How many goals is that, Mum?' asked Spinderella.

'Lots,' said Mum.

'Loads,' said her nine brothers and sisters.

'What a family!' Spinderella sighed. 'How

will I *ever* learn about numbers?'

When all the children had gone home, Spinderella said, 'Why don't *we* play football?'

'Don't be silly, we haven't got a ball,' said one of her brothers.

'I can see a little pea on the floor,' said Spinderella. 'We can use that.'

Perfect!

Mum was the ref with a whistle made

from a broken drinking straw. She chose

Speedy and Scrabble as the captains of

each team.

Speedy was the fastest runner, so nearly

all the other spiders decided to join his

team. That team scored all the goals.

'It's not fair!' the spiders on Scrabble's team started shouting.

'Yes it is! You're just jealous!' shouted the spiders on Speedy's team.

To make things worse, the spiders hurt their legs kicking the pea!

Before long they were all quarrelling, moaning, and kicking each other instead of the pea. Mum had to blow her whistle.

'How many should we have in each
team, Mum?' asked Spinderella.

'Er . . . lots,' said Mum.

'Loads,' said her nine brothers and sisters.

'I think both teams should have the same number,' said Spinderella.

'Shut up about numbers!' shouted the others.

'I'm only trying to help,' said Spinderella. But the others all turned on her. 'Down with numbers!' they yelled.

That night Spinderella felt too sad to sleep.

When morning came, she was still awake.

'I *wish* I could learn about numbers!'

she sighed.

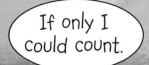

'And so you shall!' came a loud voice.

Spinderella looked up and saw an

enormous hairy spider.

'Who are you?' asked Spinderella, amazed.

'I am your Hairy Godmother,' said the

enormous spider. 'Follow me!'

The Hairy
Godmother
scuttled off
down a wall.
Spinderella
ran after her.
'Where are
we going?'
she asked.
'In here,'
said the Hairy
Godmother.

64

She ran into a classroom and up to the ceiling.

Follow me!

Keep up!

Here we are!

Below them were lots of children.

'Now, keep your eyes and ears open!'

she told Spinderella, and in a flash

she was gone.

A teacher came in with a
pile of football shirts.
'I want you to count yourselves,'
he said to the children. 'There should
be twenty of you, but let's check.'

Then came the most wonderful sound.
The children took turns to shout a
number, from one to twenty. Spinderella
swung joyfully backwards and forwards
in time to the counting.

The teacher gave
out the shirts.
'Put them on
and find the
other children
with the same
colour shirt,'
he said.
Soon there were
two groups
of children.
'How many
in each team?'
asked the teacher.

The children

counted again.

'Ten reds,' said

a girl in red.

'Ten blues,' said

a boy in blue.

'The same

number!'

shouted

Spinderella.

She was so excited that she let go of
her thread, just as the school clock
struck twelve.

'Look! A spider! Squash it!' screamed
someone. Spinderella froze in terror.

'Let's put it out of the window,' said

the teacher.

Suddenly Spinderella was outside.

'Help!' she called out, and 'Mum!'

but no one answered her.

 Two tears trickled out of

Spinderella's eyes. 'I'm lost!'

she wailed. 'I'll never see my

mum again.'

But then she looked around her.
She could see two football goals. 'It's
the playground!' she said to herself.

'The dinner hall can't be far away.'

Spinderella scuttled round

the outside of the school,

looking in all the windows.

At last she came to the dinner hall.

The window was open. Spinderella ran

inside. She rushed into the web, panting.

'I can count up to twenty!' she cried.

'Never mind about that. Eat up

your flies,' said Mum.

'I'm going to count them first,' said
Spinderella, and she did. 'I've got fourteen
flies!' she told her brothers and sisters.
'So what?' they said.

'Numbers are boring. Down with numbers! Up with flies and football!'

Who cares?

That night the spiders decided to have another football game. But once again it was a disaster, and Mum had to keep blowing her whistle.

'Mum,' said Spinderella. 'I've been counting, and there are ten of us. I think we need five spiders on each side.'

Some of the spiders muttered, 'Down with numbers!' but Mum shut them up. Spinderella sorted them into two teams of five.

Pheeeeeeeeep!

Then Mum blew her whistle for the new game to start.

This time everything was different. No one quarrelled or kicked each other.

Spinderella was in Scrabble's team, and she also helped Mum keep score.

Well done, Mum!

At half time, both teams had scored

three goals. 'Three all,' said Mum.

But still the spiders kept hurting their

spindly legs kicking the pea.

'Ow!' they said, and, 'We can't go on.'

'I *wish* we had some football boots!'

sighed Spinderella.

78

'And so you shall!' came a voice

from behind her. It was the Hairy

Godmother again!

'How many boots do you each need?'

asked the Hairy Godmother.

'Lots,' said Mum.

'Loads,' said Spinderella's brothers

and sisters.

'That's not good enough,' said the Hairy

Godmother. 'I need to have a *number*.'

'Eight!' shouted Spinderella. 'We've each got eight legs, so we each need eight boots.'

'Done!' said the Hairy Godmother.

She clapped her legs.

There was a flash.

Eight!

Well done, Spinderella!

And there on the floor of the dinner hall were ten little piles of boots. Each pile had eight boots in it. The spiders put them on and laced them up.

Then they had a wonderful second half. They scored goal after goal. The Hairy Godmother clapped and clapped.

With only a minute left to go, the score was very close, Speedy's team had eight goals, and Scrabble's team had seven. Then Scrabble scored a goal.

'It's eight all!' muttered Spinderella. 'It's going to be a draw.'

But just then the ball came her way and she gave it an almighty kick. It shot straight into the goal, just a second before her mum blew the whistle.

Spinderella had scored the winning goal!
All the spiders ran up to her. They picked
her up and cheered. 'Up with Spinderella!'
they cried. 'Up with numbers!'

If you've enjoyed these two stories, now try these!

FROM THE CREATOR OF The Gruffalo
Julia Donaldson
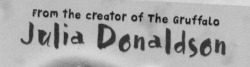

Animals in SCHOOL

Children's Laureate 2011 2010

TWO stories in ONE!

Coconut Geeky
Jill Lewis & Erica-Jane Waters

Hedgehogs Do Not Like Heights
Patricia Forde
Joëlle Dreidemy

Mairi's Mermaid
Michael Morpurgo
Illustrated by Lucy Richards

Dilly and the Goody-Goody
Tony Bradman
Illustrated by Sue Hellard